LITTLE MISS PRINCESS

Roger Hargreaves

D1392227

Written and illustrated by
Adam Hargreaves

EGMONT

Little Miss Princess' father was a King.

And her mother was a Queen.

Which, as I am sure you know, meant that
Little Miss Princess was a Princess.

And because she was a Princess she lived in a castle.

With turrets.

And a moat.

A very big castle.

And because she was a Princess she had lots of people to do everything for her.

People to mow the lawns.

People to cook her breakfast.

She even had people to make her bed.

And you would imagine that this would have made her rude and spoilt, but she was a kind and generous and good-hearted Princess.

"I am so lucky to be a Princess, I must spread my luck around," she would say to herself every morning.

And she did this by trying to help people.

She sent a chef to cook meals for Little Miss Sunshine when she heard that Little Miss Sunshine had the flu.

When she overheard Mr Busy complaining how busy he was, she sent a gardener to mow his lawn.

And she sent a maid to Little Miss Neat's house when she heard that Little Miss Neat had worn out her mop.

All of this was very useful and everyone was very grateful, but Little Miss Princess did not feel that she was really doing anything to help.

So when she heard that Mr Bump had broken his leg, she rushed round to his house to see what she could do.

"I haven't got any groceries," said Mr Bump. "You could go to the shops for me."

So Little Miss Princess went to the shops.

But because she was a Princess she had never been shopping.

She went into the bakers.

"Six sausages, please," she said to the baker.

"We don't have any sausages," said the baker.

She went into the butchers and asked for peas.

"We don't have any peas," said the butcher.

And she went into the greengrocers and asked for a loaf of bread.

"We don't have any bread," said the greengrocer.

So she went back to Mr Bump's house with an empty shopping basket.

"The shops have sold out of everything," she explained to Mr Bump.

"Everything?" said a puzzled Mr Bump.

"Yes, the butcher had no peas, the baker had no sausages and the greengrocer said he didn't have any bread."

"Ah," said Mr Bump, realising what had happened. "Why don't you try the supermarket?"

Some time later, Little Miss Princess returned with the shopping. She offered to help put everything away, but because she was a Princess she had never unpacked the shopping.

She put the sausages in the cupboard, the frozen peas in the bread bin, the bread in the drawer and …

… the milk in the oven.

Whoops!

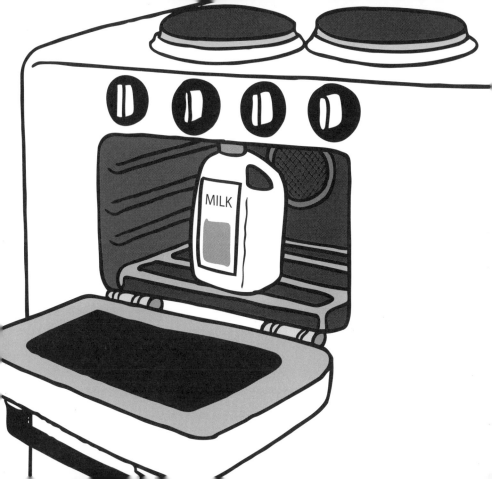

After she had put the shopping away, Little Miss Princess offered to clean Mr Bump's house, but because she was a Princess she had never cleaned anything before.

She dusted the dishes, she polished the sofa and she mopped the carpet.

Oh no!

Little Miss Princess then went upstairs to make Mr Bump's bed, but because she was a Princess she had never made a bed.

Oh dear!

Little Miss Princess then offered to cook supper for Mr Bump, but because she was a Princess she had never cooked a meal before.

For supper they had burnt sausages with burnt potatoes.

She even burnt the peas!

"Oh dear," said Little Miss Princess, throwing the burnt meal away. "I'm just no good at anything."

"Oh, I wouldn't say that," said Mr Bump. "I'm sure you are good at all sorts of things."

"Like what?" sniffed Little Miss Princess.

"I know," said Mr Bump. "Why don't you ring for a pizza?"

"What will that prove?" asked Little Miss Princess.

"Well," said Mr Bump …

" ... you are very good at giving orders!"